ready, steady, read!

The Little Green Book of the Last Lost Dinosaurs

Angie Sage

Puffin Books

PUFFIN BOOKS

Published by the Penguin Group
Penguin Books Ltd, 27 Wrights Lane, London W8 5TZ, England
Penguin Books USA Inc., 375 Hudson Street, New York, NY 10014, USA
Penguin Books Australia Ltd, Ringwood, Victoria, Australia
Penguin Books Canada Ltd, 10 Alcorn Avenue, Toronto, Ontario, Canada M4V 3B2
Penguin Books (NZ) Ltd, 182–190 Wairau Road, Auckland 10, New Zealand

Penguin Books Ltd, Registered Offices: Harmondsworth, Middlesex, England

Published in Puffin Books 1995
10 9 8 7 6 5 4 3 2

Copyright © Angie Sage, 1995
All rights reserved.

The moral right of the author/illustrator has been asserted

Filmset in Monotype Bembo Schoolbook

Reproduction by Anglia Graphics Ltd, Bedford

Printed in England by Clays Ltd, St Ives plc

Introducing Eric, one of the last
dinosaurs . . .

And the other last dinosaurs:

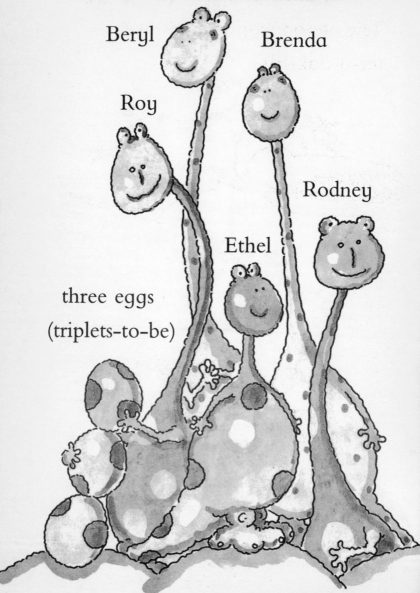

Beryl

Brenda

Roy

Rodney

Ethel

three eggs
(triplets-to-be)

Also introducing:
The pterodactyl (sounds like
ter-o-dak-til)

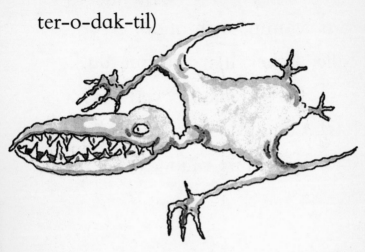

and Doreen, the dodo

Once, Eric had been an egg. He had lived in a nest on a hill next to a swamp, with another egg, called Ethel. It was a soft, dark, cosy dinosaur nest covered with lots of damp, warm leaves and splodgy swamp mud.

Beryl, Brenda, Roy and Rodney
looked after the nest and kept it
warm.

But one day there was an earthquake.

Beryl, Brenda, Roy and Rodney
disappeared down a big hole.

It took them three weeks to
climb out again.

Ethel the egg got stuck under two trees, a pile of rotting bananas and an old sock.

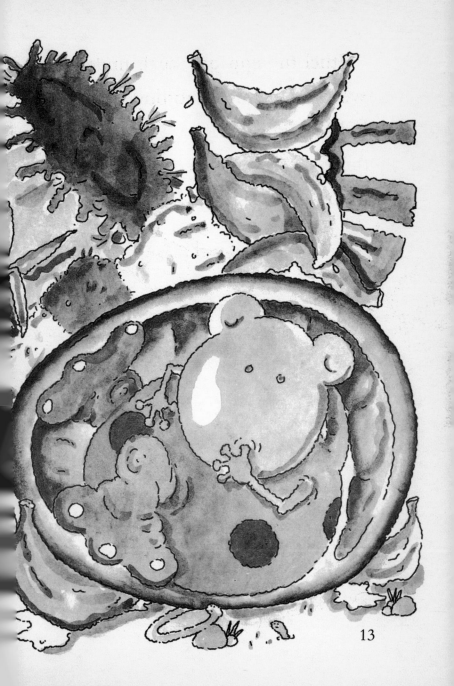

Eric the egg fell out of the nest.
Eric the egg rolled down the
hill, faster and faster. He shot
through an egg-sized gap in a
rock and out into a secret valley.

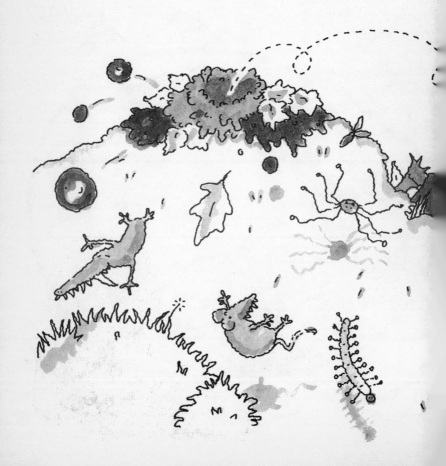

Then Eric the egg knocked over
a dodo and stopped.

Squawk!

There
goes Doreen
again

phe

The dodo, whose name was
Doreen, looked at Eric the egg.
"Ahh, little egg," she said, and sat
on him.

Three weeks later Ethel hatched,
and wriggled out from underneath
the old sock. She saw Beryl,
Brenda, Roy and Rodney climbing
out of the hole.

19

Eric hatched, and wriggled out
from underneath Doreen.

Meanwhile, Beryl, Brenda, Roy,
Rodney and Ethel were saying,
"Where's Eric?"

Beryl thought he was still in the nest, but he wasn't.

Brenda thought that some fierce dinosaurs from the next hill had kidnapped Eric.

"There aren't any other dinosaurs," said Beryl. "There's only us left."

Ethel thought he was playing hide-and-seek, but she couldn't find him.

Roy and Rodney thought that it was time for breakfast.

They all called him, just in case
they may have sat on him by
mistake, or put him in the dustbin
without noticing.

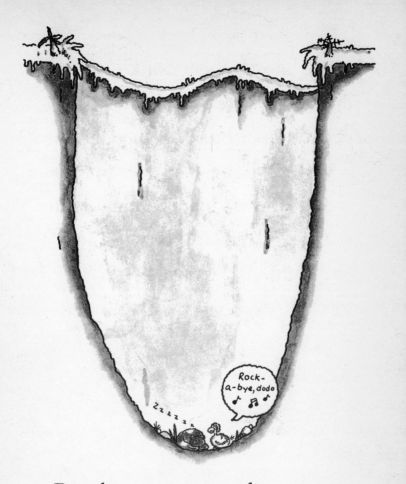

But there was no reply.

Eric was fast asleep in a dodo
nest in the secret valley on the
other side of the rock.

Now, most people think that
dinosaurs were stupid. But just
because you are very big and have
a very small head it does not mean
that you are stupid. Sometimes it
just takes a little longer to think
about things.

So it was two months and three eggs later when Beryl said, "I think Eric's lost . . . I think we should go and look for him."

Of course, if dinosaurs had really been stupid, Brenda, Roy, Rodney and Ethel would have said, "Who's Eric?"

But they didn't.

They said, "Oh."

Then they said, "Oh . . . *Eric*!"

Then they packed their tents
and sleeping-bags, put their three
new eggs in a rucksack, and went
off down the hill.

They walked through the forest,
around volcanoes, and past huge
lakes.

They were struck by lightning,
stuck in a giant spider's web and
chased by an enormous crocodile.

A few days later they were all standing in the middle of a swamp.

Roy said, "Where are we?"

Brenda said, "Look at the *map*, Roy."

Roy said, "I *am*, Brenda, but it doesn't say where we are."

"I have a feeling we've been here before," said Beryl.

"*I* know where we are!" said Ethel.

Everyone looked at Ethel. "Where?" they said.

"We're lost!" said Ethel.

There was silence while they all
thought about this.

Rodney was puzzled. "If we are
lost and Eric is lost, then why isn't
Eric here too?"

Just then a dark shadow loomed
over Ethel . . .

A pterodactyl swooped down
and snatched her up in its jaws.

Roy, Rodney, Beryl and Brenda
stood in the swamp and watched
Ethel fly away. They were not
happy.

The pterodactyl was *very* happy. He had not had any lunch for three days. He was beginning to think that he might have to eat a dodo . . . again. Dodos were too crunchy and made the pterodactyl feel sick, but juicy baby dinosaur and chips was his favourite.

Ethel was not happy.

Ethel was really scared.

She wriggled and squirmed and squeaked very loudly, "Let me go, you smelly thing!" (The pterodactyl had very bad breath.)

The pterodactyl flew up from
the swamp and over some steep
rocks. Then it saw something
wonderful. It saw another juicy
baby dinosaur just like the one
that it was going to have for
lunch. It saw Eric.

It swooped down.

Lunch *and* supper!

Eric was sitting quietly in the sun while Doreen read him a story. She had just got to a really exciting bit when . . .

The pterodactyl snatched up
Eric in his claws.

Eric yelled, "Mum!"

Doreen grabbed hold of Eric's
foot.

All the other dodos grabbed
hold of bits of Eric too.

Ethel saw her chance. She
wriggled out of the pterodactyl's
jaws and as she fell she hit his nose
THWAPP! with her tail.

The pterodactyl hopped around
holding its nose.

By doze,
by doze!

The pterodactyl had had
enough. He decided on dodo stew,
again. He dropped Eric and picked
up Doreen.

Meanwhile, back at the swamp, there was trouble.

Beryl, Brenda, Roy and Rodney were still gazing at the sky, wondering if Ethel might come back.

They had not noticed that they were sinking.

They did not notice until Roy wanted a bar of chocolate from his rucksack.

45

At that moment, who should fly past but Doreen . . .

And the pterodactyl.

The pterodactyl looked down and saw . . . *four* baby dinosaurs in the swamp.

He spat out Doreen.

Doreen landed in the mud.

The pterodactyl landed next to Beryl and pulled at her head.

"Get off, you stinky thing!" yelled Beryl. "We've got enough trouble as it is!"

The pterodactyl kept pulling and pulling.

Beryl's neck got longer and longer.

The pterodactyl pulled harder and harder.

PLOP! Beryl shot out of the mud like a cork out of a bottle. She landed on the pterodactyl and squashed him flat. SPLAT!

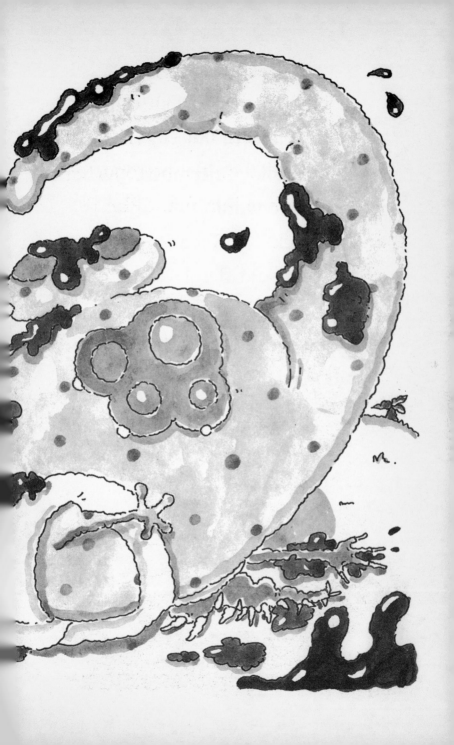

"Get us out!" yelled Roy, Rodney and Brenda to Beryl.

Beryl folded her arms. "What's the magic word?"

"Quick!" gurgled Rodney.

"No," said Beryl, "try again."

"Now!" spluttered Brenda.

Roy knew better. "Please!" he said nicely.

"Please, *what*?" asked Beryl.

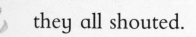

"PLEASE, DEAR BERYL!" they all shouted.

Four muddy dinosaurs, three muddy eggs and one muddy dodo sat beside the swamp.

Roy looked in his rucksack for the chocolate and found the eggs. They were beginning to crack.

The eggs hatched.

Doreen snuffled. "I had one like that once."

"What, one just like that?" asked Beryl.

"Just like that. Lovely he was."

"Oh . . . " said Beryl, and she started thinking.

Beryl was still thinking when Eric and Ethel reached the top of the huge rock that divided the secret valley from the swamp.

Eric was still saying, "But I'm a dodo," and, "I want my mum."

Ethel was saying, "No you're not, Eric, you're a dinosaur," and, "Don't worry, Eric, we'll find your mum, only she's not your mum, cos your mum's a dinosaur."

Then Eric was saying, "But I'm a dodo," and, "I want my mum."

Then there was another earthquake.

The rock shook and threw Eric and Ethel off.

They fell down, down, down, towards Beryl, Brenda, Roy, Rodney, Doreen and the triplets, who had all been sitting at the bottom of the rock for quite some time.

Doreen had just explained for the tenth time about Eric, and Beryl had just told Doreen again about Ethel and the pterodactyl, when Eric and Ethel dropped straight past them and landed in the swamp. SPLUTT!

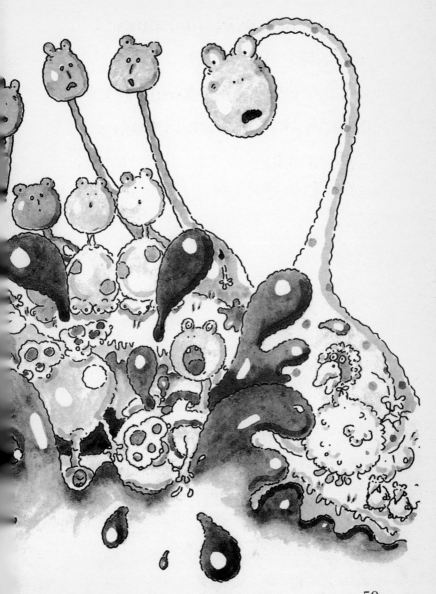

The earthquake became stronger.

The ground shook and shuddered and the rocks were thrown apart.

The swamp gathered itself up
and rushed through the space
between the rocks, taking with it
nine dinosaurs and a dodo.

It left them in a muddy pile
inside the secret valley.

As the earthquake died away the rocks moved back together and the secret valley closed up again, for ever.

And so even today in the secret valley there are still dodos and dinosaurs. But no one has seen any pterodactyls for a very long time.

ready, steady, read!

Other books in this series